The Day
the Fifth Grade
Disappeared

Other Apple Paperbacks
that you might enjoy:

The Day the Fifth Grade Disappeared

Terri Fields

AN
APPLE
PAPERBACK

SCHOLASTIC INC.
New York Toronto London Auckland Sydney

To Julia Rose Kirsch
a very special girl

With thanks to my favorite critics

Donna Cook, Barbara Bernstein,
Barbara Chriss, Rick, Lori, and Jeff Fields

No part of this publication may be reproduced in whole or in part, or stored in a retrieval system, or transmitted in any form or by any means, electronic, mechanical, photocopying, recording, or otherwise, without written permission of the publisher. For information regarding permission, write to Scholastic Inc., 730 Broadway, New York, NY 10003.

ISBN 0-590-45403-X

12 11 10 9 8 7 6 5 4 3 2   2 3 4 5 6 7/9

Printed in the U.S.A.   28

First Scholastic printing, October 1992

1

I ran from Room 5A as fast as I could. I knew there were rules about running in the hall, but sometimes when there was something really important, rules just had to be broken. Most of the time the fifth graders were really glad to be a long way from the prying eyes of Mrs. Flannery, but today, I wished the principal's yucky old secretary were right next door.

I cut across the playground and, as I hurried down the first-grade wing toward the office, I heard some little kids singing the alphabet song. I knew I had to get help fast or else there might not be any big *or* little kids left at Sandhill Elementary School.

I saw the bright orange door marked OFFICE, and I threw it open, rushing in. "Mrs. Flannery!" I started to shout. The principal's secretary never gave me a chance to get any further. She glared at me through steel-rimmed glasses. "Julia Rose Johnston." Her voice was icy cold and as mean as she could make it. "That is not an acceptable way to come into this office. Leave and try it again."

"But . . ."

"Don't argue with me, Julia."

"But you don't understand . . ."

Mrs. Flannery's face began to turn red. "No, Julia Rose, you are the one who doesn't seem to understand. I will not speak to children who are rude and who cannot obey simple rules. Now go and come back the right way!"

I had to have help, and it seemed like the fastest way to get it was to stop arguing with Mrs. Flannery, so I quickly walked out the office door and walked in again. "Mrs. Flannery," I said.

"Julia Rose, I don't care if you think you are the smartest girl in the fifth grade. You have to fill out a slip just like everyone else. Even the third graders know the procedure." She sort of sprayed saliva like a snake hissing when she said procedure. "Write down why you are here, and leave the paper on my desk."

The black-haired principal's secretary, whom the fifth grade had secretly named Dragon Lady, turned back to her computer. "But this is an emergency," I pleaded. "Honest."

"Uh-huh, they all are. Fill out the slip."

My hand was shaking, but I took the pencil and in big block letters I wrote, *MISS KENDRICK HAS FAINTED AND THE REST OF THE FIFTH GRADE HAS JUST DISAPPEARED. HELP!*

I handed the paper to Mrs. Flannery. "I said that you were to just put it on my desk, and I would . . ." Mrs. Flannery's beady blue eyes swept across the page. "Oh, my!" she interrupted herself. "Oh, dear." She glared even harder at me. "Is this the truth?"

"Of course, it's the truth! What are we going to do?"

Mrs. Flannery sniffed. "WE are not going to do anything. I know all about you fifth graders and your silly jokes. I'm warning you, if this is some kind of foolishness, you can forget about having any recess for the rest of the year."

"It's not — "

Mrs. Flannery wouldn't even let me finish. She pointed a long red nail at me. "You are going to go sit on that principal's bench until I return, and then we'll discuss it."

Mrs. Flannery, who also served as the school nurse, except on Tuesdays and Thursdays when we had a real nurse, took a black bag from her desk drawer, threw one last glare in my direction, and hurried from the office.

I didn't want to stay on the hard brown bench outside the principal's office. I wanted to go help. It might be just like in *Monty and the Angry Aliens* when weird gray and green creatures swooped out of the sky, scooped five people up in a bright silver saucer, and took off. None of the people were ever seen again.

"Lori! Jeff!" I said half aloud, thinking of my two best friends. "I don't want aliens to get you!" I could feel my heart pound and my eyes start to sting.

"Wait!" I told myself. "That was only a book. There are no such things as aliens!" But then what else could explain how the whole class just disappeared in a second?

I closed my eyes and tried to remember everything that had happened just before there was no more fifth grade. Miss Kendrick had been talking about science. She was reviewing for the test on minerals, but I figured I already knew that stuff. I started thinking about what kind of science project I could do to win the science fair. I had been kind of staring at my paper, and all of a sudden I had looked up to see Miss Kendrick falling to the floor, and the whole rest of the classroom empty.

It was unbelievably spooky. Everyone's books were still on their desks. Even Jeff's red backpack, which he never left, was still slung over the back of his empty chair. A funny feeling in my stomach was getting worse by the minute.

If only I had been paying more attention to Miss Kendrick and less to my daydream! Why didn't Mrs. Flannery come back? What was taking her so long? Suddenly, I gasped. What if Mrs. Flannery had gotten to the room, and then she'd disappeared, too? I gulped and hopped off the bench, knowing I had to at least try and save the fifth grade.

My heart was pounding as I ran down the first-grade wing and back across the playground toward Room 5A. As I got closer, I had no idea what I would find. "Hang on, Jeff; I'm coming Lori," I called to my missing two best friends. "Somehow, I'll find you wherever you went!"

I was getting close to the doorway to my classroom, and I felt my stomach begin to jump up and down inside me. When I had last left Room 5A, my favorite teacher was lying on the floor, and every kid's desk was empty. Books, papers, pencils, jackets — they were all still there, but all the kids were missing. I took a deep breath. Who knew what was waiting for me. "Please don't let me disappear forever," I whispered as I bit my lip and flung open the door.

2

"I don't believe it," I said softly staring into the room. Lori and Jeff were both back in their usual seats. In fact, absolutely everyone but me was exactly where they belonged. Miss Kendrick was standing in front of the class with a social studies book in her hand. But her face was real white, and the smile on her face didn't look like her normal smile at all. I stood in the doorway and rubbed my eyes to make sure they were seeing okay.

No one said anything to me. It was real quiet. Was this some kind of weird joke? Then I saw Mrs. Flannery, and she saw me. She pushed her steel-rimmed glasses up onto her mass of black hair and stalked toward me. Her high heels on the floor sounded like little knives as she walked. When she got to me, she bent over so that her fierce blue eyes met my hazel ones. "Julia, you will come with me, *right now!*" It wasn't a request or anything. It was a command.

"But . . ."

"And don't say one word," Mrs. Flannery ordered.

I tried to catch Lori's eye as I headed from the door. She looked scared. Of course, I couldn't be sure whether she was scared because she knew something about what had just happened, or whether she was scared because I was about to be led away by an angry witch of a school secretary.

Mrs. Flannery's high heels and my tennis shoes took us slowly back to the front office. Things did not look good. Not only did Mrs. Flannery probably not believe me about my friends disappearing, but she had positive proof that I had gotten off the principal's bench without permission. I really wanted to explain that I had only tried to help, but everything I had said so far had turned out so messed up, I was afraid to say another word.

When we got to the office, Mrs. Flannery straightened some papers on her desk that were already straight, cleared her throat a couple of times, and took out a big black book. I just stood there getting more and more confused and upset, but I knew better than to ask Mrs. Flannery when she was going to talk to me. Finally, she cleared her throat a third time and, laying her steel-rimmed glasses on her desk, she said, "Julia Rose."

I wanted to tell her that no one, I mean absolutely no one, used my middle name, but somehow I didn't think this was the time. "Yes, ma'am, I'm sorry about leaving the bench. I know you said not to, but — "

"I will speak," she interrupted coldy. "You will listen." Mrs. Flannery opened her big black book. The title was, *The Policies and Rules of the Clear Creek Unified School District*. She pointed at a place on page thirty-two with a long, pointy red fingernail. "Read this aloud," she commanded.

" 'Students are not to run on the school grounds. It disrupts classes in session, and it can be dangerous. . . .' " I looked up from the book. "Mrs. Flannery, I know those rules. I didn't run *to cause trouble;* I ran because my friends *were in trouble.* They had all, or at least I thought they had all, disappeared."

Mrs. Flannery leaned over the book and fixed me with a look that could easily decalcify a spine. "Julia Rose, I want you to listen to me very carefully. Miss Kendrick said that she did feel faint for a minute or two. Perhaps, you became frightened when you saw your teacher feeling distressed, and you let your imagination run wild."

"But — "

Mrs. Flannery cut me off. "Now, Julia Rose, you know you have a very active imagination. Even your teacher, Miss Kendrick, says so."

That wasn't what Miss Kendrick had said at all.

She said I was the most creative fifth grader she knew, but she did not ever say my imagination was too active.

Mrs. Flannery continued, "You may have thought you saw the children disappear; however, you were plainly wrong. For as you could certainly see when you disobeyed me and returned to your classroom, no students were missing. Each of them was in his or her seat learning social studies, which is what you should be doing."

"But they *were* gone. It wasn't my imagination because first, I looked around the room and saw that everyone had disappeared, and then I looked at Miss Kendrick, and then she fainted." My voice got louder as I spoke. "I am not a liar, and I wasn't imagining things. I don't understand what happened, but I do know that Miss Kendrick fainted because she saw all the kids in the class just *poof* — disappear."

Mrs. Flannery picked up a ruler that had been sitting on her desk. I moved back, sure that she was about to hit me with it, but she only tapped it on the tabletop. She spoke in clipped words like the beat of the ruler. "Julia Rose, let me make sure we understand each other." The Dragon Lady's eyes gleamed evilly, "Schools run on rules. Children are not ever supposed to break those rules. You knew that, but you broke them anyway."

Oh, boy, I thought to myself, here it comes. I

was about to lose all privileges for the rest of the fifth grade. I would be sitting in the office while everyone else had recess. Not only would I no longer be a Double Dutch champ but, pretty soon, I wouldn't even know any of the playground stuff that went on at school.

Mrs. Flannery's eyes never left mine. There was a terrible silence for a minute, and then she said, "However, I do suppose that it might be very traumatic for a child such as yourself to see her teacher almost faint." She cleared her throat. "Therefore, providing that you never speak another word about children disappearing or reappearing, you will only have to serve a recess detention today, and then you may have full privileges."

"Really? Thanks!" I said, feeling relieved about recess. I should have stopped at that. I knew it. I did. But I just had to ask because there was a part of me that just had to know. When my mother would say that I was just very naturally curious, my grandfather would shake his head and warn me that curiosity had killed the cat. Still, I took a deep breath. "Uhh, Mrs. Flannery, uh, were the kids in their seats when you first got to Room 5A?"

"Julia Rose," she thundered, and her eye twitched. "I thought we just agreed that the subject was not EVER going to be discussed again." Then her voice got real soft. "Julia, you do like recess, don't you?"

"Uh-huh," I said warily.

"And you wouldn't like to stay in every day and sit on the principal's bench when you could be playing with your friends, would you?"

"No."

"Well, then, Julia, you had better remember our agreement." Mrs. Flannery's face forced a funny kind of smile. "Really, I am just trying to help you. If you persist in telling these foolish stories about everyone disappearing when they are obviously all right here, the other children will begin to laugh at you, and pretty soon you will have no friends. Now, go back to your classroom and, if you pay attention to what you are learning, you won't have time to make up stories about things that never happened."

Mrs. Flannery dismissed me to go back to class but, just as I was about to leave the office, she called, "Julia."

I turned to face her. "Yes."

Her eyes met mine and, staring unblinkingly at me, she said, "I do hope we understand each other." There was a strange tone in the Dragon Lady's voice.

"Yes, ma'am," I replied. Actually, I didn't understand anything at all. But I knew I wanted to be out of that office. As I walked out the door, I could feel Mrs. Flannery's angry stare burning into my back.

11

3

I walked back to my classroom slowly. The kids in Mrs. Lansing's 1A class were cutting stuff out of construction paper. In Mr. Corrigan's 3C class, they were taking a spelling test. Every room I passed was filled with kids doing the stuff kids always do at school. To someone who didn't know better, it certainly looked like a perfectly normal day at Sandhill, but I wasn't sure school would ever seem quite the same to me again.

Reaching my own classroom, I almost wondered if all the kids would be missing again; you know, missing for me, then back again every time I got help. Sighing, I opened the door. Everyone was right where they belonged. I walked slowly toward my seat in the third row. Usually, Miss Kendrick said something nice to a student coming back to class, but today my teacher ignored me. As I sat down, I tried to catch Lori's eye, but she wouldn't even look at me. What was going on?

I could see that everyone still had their social

studies book out, so I pulled mine out of my desk. Miss Kendrick was talking about the mysteries of the ancient pyramids. I wanted to raise my hand and say, "Uh, excuse me, but don't you think we ought to be working on the mystery that happened right here this afternoon?" But I didn't say a word; I was too unsure of what was going on in this room.

As ordered by Mrs. Flannery, I spent my afternoon recess on the principal's hard brown bench in the office. Why Mr. MacCurrent wanted a dragon lady as his secretary was more than I could figure out. Mr. MacCurrent was a nice principal but, ever since he had had his heart attack last month, Mrs. Flannery had been practically running the school. It seemed to me that the whole place was more depressing with her in charge.

Even after my official time on the bench was up, I had to wait for Mrs. Flannery to give me permission before I could go back to class, and naturally, she made sure that recess had completely ended and everyone was already back in class before she dismissed me. That way, I would have to walk into class late, and it would remind everyone that I had missed recess. Honestly, no one could just accidentally be that mean. She had to practice. I tried to imagine Mrs. Flannery sitting at home deciding what mean things she could do to kids for the next week.

At least there wasn't much time left before the

dismissal bell rang. At last, I could rush over to Lori's desk. Almost at the same exact time, we both looked at each other and said, "What happened to you today?"

"What happened to me?" I exclaimed. "Hey, I just went to the office. Where did you go?"

Lori looked at me. She brushed her bangs away from her eyes. "Go? Where did I go? I didn't go anywhere except to recess."

By this time, Jeff had zipped his red backpack and, before I could say any more, he walked over to us, and said, "Hi, how come the two of you are looking at each other so weird?" And then he grinned. "Or maybe it's just that you have both gotten weirder-looking. What's up?"

"Very funny, Jeff." He thought he was going to be a famous comic when he grew up and he was always saying dumb things that he thought were clever. Actually, what was weird was that Jeff and Lori and I were all still such good friends. Most of the time in the fifth grade, boys and girls pretended to hate each other, but Jeff and Lori and I had been best buddies ever since we had gone to preschool together, a long time before the boys had only hung out with the boys and the girls only with the girls. Jeff was almost like a brother who both drove me crazy and was a real important part of my life.

"OK," he said, "you didn't like that joke so well?

You're a tough audience. Try this one: Do you know why baseball players like to go to the park? Give up? They enjoy the swings!" He laughed at his own joke and then realized that neither Lori nor I were laughing with him.

"That was really dumb," Lori said.

"Ahh, that's just because you're girls. You probably don't even understand the joke. See swings are at a park, but there are also baseball swings when the batter — "

"We understand," Lori interrupted. "We just thought it was dumb."

This was unbelievable. Why were they talking about some baseball joke instead of their disappearance? Maybe something had happened to their brains while they were gone. "Uhhh . . . you guys," I said, "don't you even care that the whole school could be gone tomorrow?"

"All right! Sounds great to me," Jeff shouted. "No more homework. Guess I might as well throw this old backpack away."

"Jeff," I said, "I'm serious. I really am. Will you quit making jokes? Listen, you guys, I don't know exactly what's going on, but I think it could be pretty scary. I'm trying to make sense of this whole crazy day, and I don't see why you are just acting like everything is OK."

"Uh, gosh, we're sorry," Lori said. "We were just trying to cheer you up because you got in trouble today. Tell us what's wrong. Exactly what are you trying to make sense of and what's so scary?"

Didn't they even know they had disappeared? This was getting stranger and stranger. I decided it was all much too important to discuss anywhere but our special meeting place. "We need an emergency meeting," I said. "Right away."

"All right," Lori said. "Are you okay, Julia?"

"I don't know," I answered truthfully as we walked off of the school grounds. I saw Lori look at Jeff worriedly. Four blocks later, we were at our meeting place. A huge old oak tree, off to one side of Lori's house, it had been our fort, our store, our playhouse, and now it was our special place to meet. It was our favorite spot just to be friends. Jeff didn't have to tease us to show the guys that girls were dumb, and we didn't have to keep explaining to our girlfriends that Jeff was like a brother, not a boyfriend.

Once there, Jeff threw his backpack down on the ground and plopped himself down under the shadiest part of the tree. The two of us sat down next to him. "Okay," he said, "enough of this mystery stuff. Why did the Dragon Lady come after you, and what does that have to do with the school disappearing?"

I took a deep breath and said we all had to take the secret oath first. A secret oath was something Lori had read in a book when she was in third grade. She thought it was so neat that we made up our own, and we still used it on real important stuff. We each held our hand up and repeated, "I won't tell. It won't ever be me. Our secret is safe within us three."

The oath finished, Lori and Jeff sat on the blanket and waited. "Well . . . ?" Jeff said.

"Well," I said, "this may sound a little weird, but here goes." I told Lori and Jeff how I hadn't been paying attention in science because I had been daydreaming that I had just won the grand prize in this year's science fair. When my daydream ended, I looked up, and there weren't any people in the class, except me and Miss Kendrick. "We looked at each other, and then Miss Kendrick fainted. That's when I ran to get Mrs. Flannery." I told them about what Dragon Lady Flannery had done, and how I had finally hopped off the bench and come back to class, only to find everyone back in their seats.

I stopped to catch my breath. "So . . . what I want to know, is where did you go, and how did you get back?"

Lori's brown eyes met Jeff's hazel ones, and the two of them looked at each other with a strange look. Then Lori said slowly, "I know you wouldn't tease us, especially after the secret oath, but are you sure we disappeared? Honest, we didn't feel like we went anywhere. Wouldn't we have known if we were gone?"

17

I scratched my head. "Maybe whoever made you disappear erased your memory or something. I don't know. But I do know absolutely for sure positive that you did disappear. Gone! *Poof*! *Zap*! Really!"

Jeff looked at me. He was wearing a Dodger baseball hat, and he turned it around backward. "Let's see if I understand. We went somewhere, but we didn't know we left; we didn't know when we got back, and we never even knew that we were gone. Now, that's weirder than any joke that I could ever come up with."

Lori's brown eyes grew large, and she said excitedly, "Oh, you guys, just think. A real mystery right here. This is better than anything on TV. Julia, maybe this mystery is going to make us all real famous. How are we going to solve it?"

Both Lori and Jeff turned toward me. I was relieved that they believed me, but I had no idea how to solve the mystery. "Well," I said, playing with the ribbon on my pigtail, "I'm not sure, but I'll try to think of a plan for us."

Jeff tried to joke, but his voice didn't sound very joking when he said, "Yeah, we'll plan to make the mystery disappear, while someone out there plans to make us disappear."

Put that way, it wasn't quite as exciting. In fact, it was probably just because a little wind had started blowing, but suddenly, I felt cold, and I noticed that Jeff and Lori were shivering.

18

4

At that moment, Lori's mom stuck her head out the door and yelled that we were all supposed to head to our houses for dinner. "Let's meet back here at seven," I suggested.

"Okay, and don't say a word to anyone else! This is OUR mystery to solve!" Lori added.

During dinner my mom asked me if I was getting sick because she'd never seen me so quiet, but I told her I was just thinking. As soon as I cleared the table, I pulled on a sweatshirt and told Mom that I was going back to Lori's. On the way to her house, I started to think how neat it would be if we really could solve this mystery. Probably we would get interviewed on television! I could almost see us watching a TV show and hearing, "Julia Johnston and her best friends, Lori Shelle and Jeff Leonard, have just saved our city. Tune in at ten P.M. for details!"

As I turned the corner, I could see that Jeff and Lori were already waiting at the tree. When

19

I got there, Lori said that they had been talking about how it would be when we solved the whole mystery. "Jeff and I decided that if one of us has to talk to a reporter, you can do it, Julia, because you know how to use the most big words."

"Yeah," Jeff said, "but be sure to tell them I do good jokes."

Lori had brought a big bag of Oreo cookies, some paper, and pens. She turned to me, "Okay, I've got the supplies. You know, I've never worked on a real mystery before. Tell us again. Exactly what did it look like when we were all gone?"

As I described the room once more, I tried to put in every detail. I said, "Remember when we had the fire drill and we had to rush out of the room leaving everything exactly in its place? Well, that's how it looked. It was real quiet, too. Then Miss Kendrick fainted." I sighed. "Gosh, I wish you guys could remember something about what it was like when you were gone."

"Me, too," said Jeff.

Lori shook her head. "It's all so strange. What happened to us?"

I tilted my head as I thought. "Well, I didn't see you disappear, and I didn't see you come back. You guys don't remember the whole thing, so we're going to have to talk to someone else for some clues."

"Yeah? Like who?" Jeff asked.

I started counting on my fingers. "Well, for starters, Mrs. Flannery, because she may know something important."

Jeff whistled softly, "I'd rather capture six black widow spiders alive than spend ten minutes with her."

"Me, too," Lori said, "She's like a thousand black widow spiders. Besides, even if she knew something, she would never tell us."

"You're probably right," I said, "but I still think we have to find a way to talk to her. Either you guys were back by the time she got to our class, and she thinks I'm nutty — "

Jeff broke in, "Or we weren't there, and she saw us reappear!"

We all thought about that. Lori took an Oreo, split it in two parts, and said, "Wow! Even Mrs. Flannery must have been a little freaked out. I'll bet she didn't have a single rule to cover that!"

"Yeah," said Jeff, "and how do you know that that old witch wasn't the one who made us disappear in the first place?!"

Jeff's point was a good one and, for a few minutes, no one said anything. Finally, I took a deep breath. "Well, even if she did, the only way we'll ever know for sure is by talking to her until we can get her to slip up somehow."

I took a bite of my Oreo. "You know we can't

forget Miss Kendrick either. She must have seen something before she fainted. Otherwise, why would she have fainted?"

"I'll talk to Miss Kendrick," Lori offered.

"Oh, yeah? What are you going to say?" Jeff asked her. "Excuse me, Miss Kendrick, but have very many of your classes just sort of faded away before your eyes?"

Lori said she really didn't think it was Miss Kendrick because our teacher liked us all too much to want the class to be gone.

I thought Lori was probably right, but I decided our investigation better make sure of everything. "Listen, you guys," I said, "until we know, we suspect everyone and trust no one. After all, we're never going to get famous if we don't get the mystery solved."

Jeff nodded. "Agreed. It could be anybody. What I'm thinking about is why? I mean what does someone want to do with us?" There were only a few stars in the sky, and both Lori and I jumped when Jeff moved his hand on the blanket and crushed some of the oak leaves beneath it.

The three of us huddled a little closer together and continued to plan. We discussed, debated, and decided. And by eight-fifteen, when we had to leave for home, we felt sure we had the method to find out just how the fifth grade had disappeared.

5

When I crawled in bed that night, I stuffed the notes and plans we had made at Lori's into the question pad under my bed. I figured I should save everything because, when we cracked the case and became famous, lots of people would want to see our notes. I knew I would never be able to sleep, because I was so excited, but the day must have worn me out because I remember staring up at my ceiling, and the next thing I knew my mother was standing over me the following morning warning that this was her absolute last wake-up call.

I jumped out of bed and looked in my closet carefully. I wanted to wear just the right thing today. I wanted to look grown-up, for I had been given the job of talking to Mrs. Flannery. I wasn't sure what I was going to say since she had forbidden me to talk about *the incident,* but I figured it would help if I looked more grown-up when we talked. My closet is not exactly the perfect place for grown-up outfits since I really like jeans and neon T-shirts, but I do have one green and white dress that my mom said makes me look at least thirteen. Mom gets all teary-eyed every time I put it on, which isn't often! Today, I took it from my closet, hoping it might have even one hundredth of the effect on Mrs. Flannery that it has on my mom!

Wolfing down a bowl of Cheerios, I got to school just before the warning bell rang. I slid into my seat and gave Jeff and Lori a thumbs-up sign.

I had decided that there was no point to my trying to talk to Mrs. Flannery until school was out. If she was going to say anything other than "Get back to class!" I'd have to wait until she knew I didn't have any class. Of course, that didn't mean the day was a waste. Lori, Jeff, and I had agreed that, since school was the easiest for me out of all of us, I would be the one to take side notes on anything unusual at all that Miss Kendrick did or said just in case she did something special right before everyone disappeared.

At recess, Lori put her part of the plan into action. Pretending to look for a lost paper, she sat at her desk until all the other students had filed out the door. I stood outside just long enough to watch her walk to the front of the class and say, "Miss Kendrick, I was thinking of being a fifth-grade teacher when I grew up, and I wondered if any weird things ever happened to you; while you were teaching that is."

Jeff had headed out to the playground. On the chance that whatever controlled the class had occurred from outside the room, Jeff was to figure out whether anything was even slightly unusual or out of place under the window of our classroom.

While Jeff searched the playground, and Lori pumped Miss Kendrick for information, I went to the library. The librarian was used to me stopping in and greeted me with a big smile. "Well, Julia, what are we interested in reading today?"

"Uh . . . actually, I'm thinking of doing a report on strange disappearances."

The librarian tapped her pencil on the card catalog. "Strange disappearances? I'm not sure you'll find anything under that category."

The librarian was wrong, and she was right. I did find two books on disappearing, but one was a magic book, and the other one talked about what to do if you got lost. As recess ended, I hoped that Lori or Jeff had had better luck than I had.

At lunch, we tried to talk about it without saying anything too suspicious. Lori and I asked the girls at our lunch table if they ever wished they could just evaporate from school, and Jeff was supposed to be bringing the same thing up to the boys to see if anyone reacted.

Jeff had after-school baseball, which he never

missed for any reason, and I still had to face going in to talk to Mrs. Flannery, so Lori said she would go home and get her piano practicing out of the way. Last night, we had agreed not to say a word to each other until all three of us could hear what we had found at the same time. That's why we decided on a five P.M. meeting under Lori's tree for today.

The clock on our classroom wall was right above a bulletin board about Halloween, and I watched the last few minutes of the day tick away, glancing first at the clock and then at the witch on the bulletin board. The witch only reminded me of what I was about to face. Still, Lori and Jeff were counting on me, so when the school dismissal bell rang, I took a deep breath and headed for old Dragon Lady's office.

I walked in and signed my name on a slip of paper. Why she needed the dumb things, I'll never know because she never even looked at mine before she said, "Yes, Julia, I trust you are having no more problems, so exactly what is it you need today?"

"I . . . uh . . . I don't really need anything." I took a deep breath. What good had it done to wear this teenager dress if Mrs. Flannery wouldn't even look up and see that I had it on. I took another deep breath and plunged on. "I just wanted to come by to say . . . uh . . . I uhm, I'm sorry about yesterday."

The good news was that I did manage to con Mrs. Flannery into letting me stay around the office and "help" her for an hour. The bad news was that I spent the whole hour tearing carbon papers out of old forms. Mrs. Flannery refused to make any conversation, and no one came in the office, so I didn't learn one thing.

I went home to change my clothes and, once in an old pair of jeans and my favorite purple T-shirt, I headed for our tree. I realized that for all my work, I had absolutely nothing to report. I didn't know one thing more that would help explain how or why the fifth grade had vanished. I could only hope that Lori and Jeff had had better luck.

6

I was the first one at our meeting spot, but it was only a few minutes before Lori and Jeff got there, too. Jeff was carrying a big bag of Doritos. "Hi, guys," he said between bites. "So who's asking me about practice today?" Without waiting for an answer, he continued, "I hit a ball that would have gone forever, if that dumb gray fence just hadn't been there to stop it. I wish they'd never built the stupid building next door to school. Then we could still have a big enough baseball field." With that, Jeff sighed and plopped down on the ground. "What's new with our mystery?"

Lori sat down more gently. "I really found out a lot from Miss Kendrick!"

"You did!" I exclaimed. Suddenly, my tiredness from the whole day disappeared. "Wait a minute, and I'll take notes on our official notepad."

Lori bit her lip. "Actually, I don't think you'll have to do that. I mean I found out tons of interesting stuff about her being a teacher and all, but now that I think about it, Miss Kendrick didn't really say anything that would help us with the mystery."

I guess Lori saw my disgusted look because she added, "But I tried, honest. I kept asking about weird things that had happened to her while she was teaching. Once, she started to say, 'Well, yesterday . . .' but then she stopped and said, 'Really, there's nothing weird about being a teacher. It's just fun.'"

Jeff finished munching a Dorito, and then said, "Don't feel bad, Lori, I didn't do much better. It's not like I didn't work at it though. The guys wanted to play basketball during recess, but I said I couldn't. I felt the wall outside our room for secret passages. I checked the playground under our window to see if there were any secret openings, but there were none. Shoot, I even told some little kids I lost my pet invisible bug, and they offered to help me look for it. At least that was funny!"

"Jeff, that was mean!" I said.

"Oh, yeah?" he said, munching another Dorito. "Well, what did *you* find out?"

I filled them in about the library, and the three of us looked at our investigation pad. It was one big zero.

I wish I could say that things got better from there, but they didn't. I spent three more boring afternoons in the office with the Dragon Lady, who still never even bothered to say thank you for all the work I had done. We found no more clues, got no new ideas, and the 5A class went on boringly normal. They never even half-faded away again. Lori and Jeff quit talking about *when* we solved the mystery and started saying *if* we ever solved it.

Soon it had been almost two weeks since the fifth grade had disappeared and, as the three of us met under the tree, I took out our now worn investigation pad. "Does anyone have anything to add today?"

Silence was the answer. Jeff was lying on his back, looking up at the sky through the tree branches. He yawned. "Julia, this one's for you. There are these two kids, and the first one says to the other one, 'Knock, knock.' The second one says, 'Who's there?' And the first one says, 'Howell.' 'Howell who?' 'Howell we ever know when this investigation is supposed to be over?' "

Lori groaned. "Not that I think Jeff's funny, but he does have a point. There's just nothing to find around Sandhill. We only disappeared for a minute or so, and it happened a long time ago now. I really wanted to solve a mystery. I wanted it to be something super exciting, but we talked to kids and teachers, checked the classroom and the playground, and everything is a big zero. No one ever disappeared since that day, so maybe it's just one of those *Twilight Zone* deals we weren't meant to solve."

"But what about never knowing the answer to what happened to you? What about our all getting to be famous?" There was silence in return to my questions.

My friends were finished with this mystery. And after all, who could blame them? They still didn't quite believe they had ever disappeared in the first place and, in all this time, I hadn't been able to provide even one tiny reason to keep investigating. "Okay," I said softly. "You guys have been great detectives. Thanks."

I should have been relieved. The end of our being detectives meant that I didn't have to see Mrs. Flannery anymore. I didn't have to try to keep track of everything that was going on in the classroom. I didn't have to try to keep Lori and Jeff convinced that they had disappeared. I could just forget the whole thing. I told myself I was glad, but I wasn't. It was just something about me. If there was a question, I wanted an answer. If there was a mystery, I wanted a solution.

But instead of getting solutions, all I managed to get was a cold. The next day I woke up with a nose that was sniffly and a throat that was scratchy. I just felt blah, but I went to school because I didn't want to stay home, lie in bed, and think about the investigation that failed.

All morning my nose went between being real stuffy and running. Finally, in math, I raised my hand and asked Miss Kendrick if I could go get a drink of water. "All right," she said, "but please come right back."

I stepped outside the door, blew my nose, which sounded like a barking seal, and walked to the drinking fountain. The icy cold water felt really good on my sore throat. I wanted to just stand in the hallway and keep drinking more water, but I had promised Miss Kendrick I would hurry back, so I returned to class. I opened the door and started for my seat. "Oh, no!" I gasped. "I don't believe it. Not again."

My heart started pounding real hard. There was only one door to our classroom, and no one but me had gone through it, yet the entire classroom was empty. I ran to the front of the room to see if Miss Kendrick had fainted again, but this time, Miss Kendrick was gone, too!

I didn't know what to do, but I did know what I wasn't going to do. I wasn't going to get Mrs. Flannery and I wasn't going to leave this class-room. Whatever clues there were would be happening right here.

"All right, think!" I said aloud to the empty classroom. I looked at the clock. It might be important to know exactly what time the class had disappeared. I took a piece of chalk and wrote on the board, ten-thirty A.M. Then I thought, I've got to make Lori and Jeff really believe that they were gone this time. I ran over to Jeff's desk and took his red backpack from his chair. I switched it with Greg Smythe's green backpack, knowing that in a million, zillion years, Jeff would never give Greg his backpack. Then I switched three or four other backpacks. That way, Jeff couldn't be blamed.

"Okay," I told myself. Time to start looking for clues. I started at the row by the door and stared real hard at each part of the classroom piece by piece, but everything looked exactly the same as always. It wasn't fair. In mystery books, detectives were always able to find clues.

Maybe I just wasn't looking in the right places. I ran up behind Miss Kendrick's desk to see things from where she sat. Nothing unusual from that way either. Then I turned around. On the wall behind her desk, Miss Kendrick had a picture of George Washington crossing the Delaware. All of a sudden, I got excited. That picture was the only removable thing on the walls of our room. Maybe Miss Kendrick had hung it there to cover up a secret mirror or something. Anxiously, I took George down, but there was only a nail and a blank wall behind the picture. I sighed with discouragement. When I rehung the picture, I put it upside down. At least it was one more thing to let Lori and Jeff know that the class had disappeared.

It was getting pretty creepy being the only one

in this room. I wished that everybody would come back. The class had been gone almost five minutes now, and I stood in the front of the room watching. How would it happen? Would kids start coming back a few at a time? Would they begin materializing like shadows and then become real people? Then I got that terrible sort of sick-in-the-stomach feeling as I realized that, maybe this time, they weren't coming back at all!

7

I sat down in Miss Kendrick's empty desk. Boy, what good did it do to get straight A's, to have a big gold trophy for having been the most outstanding student in the fourth grade, if you never learned anything that could help you in case of a real emergency? I felt like a total failure.

It had now been ten minutes, and the class still hadn't come back. As far as I could see there were absolutely no clues and no reasons why they had disappeared.

I walked to the door and put my hand on the knob. As much as I wanted to be here when the class reappeared again, I had to go for help. Who knew what could be happening to them wherever they were?

Leaving the classroom, I started down the hallway. Wait a minute, I thought, I ought to take a teacher's book or something with me to prove to Mrs. Flannery that Miss Kendrick wasn't in the room, that this wasn't my imagination. I ran back to our classroom.

Opening the door, I gasped. There were all my friends sitting at their desks except for Jeff and Greg who were exchanging backpacks. I stood in the doorway too amazed to move. Miss Kendrick noticed me there. "Thanks for getting your drink of water so quickly."

"Yes, ma'am," I said softly. I looked at Lori, and she looked at me questioningly. I nodded my head *yes* ever so slightly.

As I walked past her desk, she whispered, "We disappeared again, didn't we?"

"Do you know what happened to you this time?" I asked.

"No," she whispered, "but I vote that we reopen the case."

I took my seat feeling that this just might be a pretty good day after all. I had no sooner sat down than a most unusual thing happened. Mrs. Flannery, who practically never left her office, walked into our classroom. "Everything okay today?" she asked.

Miss Kendrick paused for a moment. "Uhhh . . ." Then she straightened her shoulders and looked firmly at Mrs. Flannery. "Everything's just fine. We were just finishing our math. Would you care to join us?"

"Thank you, but I promised Mr. MacCurrent

that I would stop into all the classes today, so I really must be going."

Hah! I thought to myself. Mrs. Flannery had never come around to check on all of the classes before. The Dragon Lady had to know what was going on in this room! Well, she didn't fool me for one minute, and no matter how scary she was, she wasn't going to stop me from finding out what was happening.

In the back of my mind, I was already forming an idea for after school. Then I saw a note coming across the classroom. Marsha passed it to Diane, who passed it to me. It said *"Julia"* on the front, and when I opened it, the inside read, *"Tree at three? Jeff."*

I stared at it for a minute. There was so much I wanted to tell Jeff. Then I stopped and thought. You had to be careful what you wrote in notes because they were against the rules, and if Miss Kendrick caught you, she read the note out loud. That's why I only wrote back, *"No time. Stay here."* I started to fold the note shut, and then I reopened it and quickly scribbled *"and don't say a word."*

When school was out, Jeff, who usually shot out of our room the minute the bell rang, slowly closed his backpack, opened it again, and then reclosed it looking at me. I returned his look and then I caught Lori's eye and nodded. They followed me out of the room and onto the playground. Pretty soon, Jeff said, "Okay, what's up? Geez, I can't believe we disappeared again. We've got to find some clues."

"That's why there's no time to go to the tree. The clues are here, and the best one is not going to get away this time!"

"Huh?" Jeff said. "Did I miss something?"

"Listen, you guys, don't you think it's pretty weird that Mrs. Flannery just happened to show up at our room right when she did? I mean when is the last time you can ever remember her coming to our room?" Without waiting for an answer, I rushed on. "I've been thinking about it all day; she has to be the clue. Either she made us disappear herself or she knows who did."

Lori took a deep breath. "But you tried finding out about her, Julia, and all you got for your trouble was sore hands from working in the office. There's no way to find out about her. Besides, she gives me the creeps."

"But there has to be a way. I just wasn't thinking hard enough before. I kept counting on her to talk to me and let something slip, but she isn't ever going to do that. She may be mean, but she isn't dumb."

Lori scratched her head. "I wonder why she wants to make us disappear anyway? What's it prove?"

"I don't know," I said. "Maybe she's just learning to make people disappear, and we're like a test. Maybe she can't make it last for very long yet, but she's working on it."

Lori's brown eyes were growing larger. She half whispered, "And when she can, then what?"

"Well," I said, "I'm not sure. Maybe when she can make people disappear and stay gone as long as she likes, she figures she'll be in charge of the school, and then the whole town. Anyone who doesn't like it will just disappear."

Jeff shoved his baseball cap further back on his head and fixed me with a look. "I agree that the Dragon Lady is a real jerk, but I think there's got to be some other answer. I don't see how even Mrs. Flannery could make anyone disappear."

My hazel eyes stared into his. "I don't either — yet. But we're going to follow her everywhere she goes, and I'll bet we find out pretty soon."

Although he said he didn't think it would prove anything, Jeff agreed to wait with us behind the oleander bushes in front of the school so that we could follow Mrs. Flannery when she left without her knowing it. We scrunched down in the back of the tall bushes so no one could see us. It wasn't long until our legs cramped and our backs ached from the position. My throat was still really hurting, too, but I tried not to think about it.

Finally, Jeff said, "Hey, has anyone ever seen her go home? Maybe Dragon Lady just lives at the school."

"Shhh," I said, "here she comes!" Through the bushes, we could see a tall lady in a red print dress walk out of the front door of the school. Her black hair was pulled into her usual tight bun, and her long red fingernails were clutching a bunch of papers. Her high heels clicked so loudly on the sidewalk that we could have heard her even if we couldn't have seen her.

"How far in front of us should we let her get before we go after her?" Jeff whispered. "We don't want to lose her."

I had been thinking the same thing, and I was going to suggest we start after her once she reached the end of the parking lot sidewalk, when Mrs. Flannery stopped where she was. She opened her purse, took out some keys, and unlocked a dark blue car.

I hit my head. How could I not have thought she would be driving! Just because we kids walked everywhere didn't mean adults did. "Look," Lori whispered, "she'll drive off, and then we'll never catch her!"

"Well," I said miserably, "at least we can watch which way the car goes."

As soon as Mrs. Flannery had gotten in and started the motor, we came out of the bushes. There was a red car in front of her. It made a right turn from the parking lot, and then Mrs. Flannery's car turned right, too. "Maybe she'll have to stop at the light," Jeff said, and he bolted down the sidewalk.

Lori and I hurried to catch up with him. When we did, Jeff looked very confused. Huffing and puffing, I asked, "What'd you see?"

"Look," Jeff said. The red car that had been in front of Mrs. Flannery's was stopped at the light on the corner. Mrs. Flannery's car, however, was nowhere to be seen. Jeff shook his head. "Where'd she go?"

"Well, if she went right out of the parking lot, there's no street she could have turned onto. So she had to have stopped before she got to the corner."

"Yeah," Jeff said, "or she just disappeared." He turned to me. "Now what Sherlock? Or do we just go home?" Then he grinned, "Hey, get it? Sherlock . . . Holmes. . . ."

"Jeff, not now!" I commanded. "Come on. We'll walk down to the corner and see if her car is parked somewhere. Look at everything really carefully."

I didn't really expect to see anything new. After all, we walked down this block every day. Right next door to the school was the ugly gray building that had been built just this year. It had a big fence around it, and there was barbed wire on top of that. We were told that kids were not wanted there, and any student caught anywhere around

41

it would get in big trouble. The first week it was open, Bobby Rafert tried to sneak in and got caught. He got suspended from school for it and, when he got back, he said it wasn't worth getting suspended, that it was just a bunch of dumb offices. After that, except for the baseball players who complained about losing their fields, we pretty much ignored the place.

It wasn't hard to do. Heck, it didn't even look like anything special except for the little building in front of it. Right where the cars could drive in the parking lot, there was a little building with a soldier standing next to it. When a car started into the parking lot, the guard would stop it, talk to the person, and then the person would usually turn around and leave. "Well, she can't be in here," Jeff said as we started past the building. "Nobody ever gets in, so let's hurry. Maybe Mrs. Flannery stopped at the market down the way."

Walking quickly, we peeked into the fence where the guard was. "Uhhh," Lori gasped, "look!" And we all watched as the guard waved Mrs. Flannery's blue car into the parking lot!

8

H er car turned further into the parking lot, and we couldn't see it anymore. "Well, come on!" I said.

Lori smoothed her hands on her dress. "Uhhh, come on where?"

"Into the building, where else?" I said.

"But, Julia, we can't get in there!" Lori said.

"Come on! We can try. Now look innocent." We took about two steps, then I said, "Wait a minute. One of us should stay behind, just in case . . ." I bit my lip. "Just in case the other two of us get in and don't come back out. At least then, one person can go for help."

"Maybe we ought to just tell a grown-up about this whole thing," Lori said.

I sighed. "Right! You guys barely believed me when I tried to tell you about it, and you're my best friends. What grown-up would ever believe that kids are just disappearing? Jeff, you wait out here. If we don't come back in a half hour, you run as fast as you can, and get help."

Jeff argued for a minute, but I convinced him that since he was the fastest runner, he was the best one to go get help. Lori and I left him sitting down against the wall outside the building. Then she and I walked toward the guardhouse. My grandma Barb once said we were the two most adorable little girls she had ever seen, and I hoped we would look that way to the guard. As we got close to his little house, he stepped out in front of us, and he sure looked a lot taller than he did from back on the street.

"Hey, you kids aren't supposed to be here. Now go on, take a hike before I have to report you," he said, and his voice came out deep and loud.

"Well, what is this place anyway?" Lori asked. "I just moved in here, and I've never seen a building with a guard before."

"This is a place that isn't for little kids with questions. Now scram."

"But . . ." I said, "our teacher just went in. She was driving a blue car, and I . . . uh . . . I . . . uh forgot to give her my homework. If I don't get it to her before tomorrow, it will be late, and then I'll get in trouble. Couldn't I just run in, give it to her, and I'll come right back out."

The guard almost smiled. "Blue car. Yeah, she was a pistol. Pretty mean teacher, huh?"

"Yeah," I said, thinking of Mrs. Flannery. "You can't imagine how mean."

"Well, I'll tell you what. You leave the paper with me, and when she comes out, I'll make sure she gets it."

"But . . . I . . . I . . . have to give it to her myself!"

The guard began to lose patience. "Look, you can give me the paper or you can forget it, but kids aren't supposed to be here, and I'm going to get in trouble if you don't scram. Now, what will it be?"

I knew I couldn't leave any paper with my name on it for Mrs. Flannery, and I could see that the guard wasn't going to budge. "Thanks anyway," I said, and Lori and I turned to leave.

"Kids," he muttered, watching us go.

When we got outside the building fence, we had to tell Jeff every detail. "We tried everything we could think of," I said, "but nothing worked. I wonder why the guard let Mrs. Flannery in?"

We walked in silence to the tree. When we had abandoned our investigation, I'd thrown the question/clue pad into the chest by the tree, and today, I dug it out. We looked over our old questions, and added everything we had learned. It wasn't a lot, but we did know for sure that Mrs. Flannery was doing something real suspicious and that the class had disappeared again, this time for almost fifteen minutes. We were pretty sure that the gray building was involved. "Okay," I said before we all left for home, "then we agree. We've got to find out what that gray building is, and then we've got to find out how to get into it."

That night I mentioned the gray building to my mom but she said that all she knew was that it was some kind of government facility. The next morning, I got to school a little early and asked Miss Kendrick about the gray building. "Oh, it's just some kind of U.S. Army building," she said. "When it was going up, I asked about taking all of you there for a field trip, but I was told it was just a bunch of offices. Why are you asking?"

"I don't know," I replied. "I guess, it's just that it's so ugly with that big gray fence and then all that wire on the top."

"It sure is," Miss Kendrick said. "Maybe the student council could plant some flowers by our side of the fence." With that, the first bell rang, and students started into the classroom. I struggled to keep my eyes and ears on what Miss Kendrick was doing, but my thoughts and my eyes kept wandering toward the window and the gray fence beyond. What was really going on there?

There sure were no clues here. In fact, it was a very normal day. Math went into science, lunch passed on to reading. All of a sudden, the intercom squawked and Mrs. Flannery's voice sounded very irritated. "Miss Kendrick, I called Richard Johnson to the office almost five minutes ago. His mother is waiting to take him to the eye doctor. Now is he coming or not?"

Miss Kendrick looked very confused, and so did the rest of us. "I'm sorry," Miss Kendrick said, "I didn't hear you call him."

"Didn't hear me?" she said. "I've plainly called for him twice. This makes the third time."

"Well," Miss Kendrick replied, "I guess the intercom must not be working properly because this is the first time I heard you. I'll send him right away. Please apologize to his mother."

Richard took his backpack and left. A few minutes later, the janitor came down to our room. "Mrs. Flannery asked me to check your intercom," he said.

The janitor climbed up on a ladder, removed the screws that held the metal box in place, and looked at the wires. Then he put it together again. "I'm real sorry, Miss Kendrick," he said, "but I don't see a thing wrong with your intercom. Let me know if you have any more problems, but I can't understand why you didn't hear her."

Miss Kendrick thanked the janitor, and he left shaking his head. But Lori, Jeff, and I knew why she hadn't heard the intercom. The intercom had worked just fine. It was just that she hadn't been there to hear it. Miss Kendrick and the class had disappeared again. Then my mouth dropped open as I realized that finally, this time, I must have disappeared right with them!

9

At first, I was thrilled. I had actually done it. I had disappeared and reappeared! But it was weird. I didn't feel like any time had passed at all. I didn't feel as if I had ever left my seat. So what did I know now that I hadn't known before? Nothing! Secretly, I had been sure that, if I could just disappear once, I would find some clue, but now that it had happened, I had to admit that I didn't learn one thing.

School ended without the class disappearing again. At least, I don't think it disappeared again. For I suddenly realized that we could be disappearing all the time and never know it at all!

Lori had a piano lesson, and Jeff had basketball, so I said that I would wait at school to see if Mrs. Flannery went back to the gray building. For a while I sat across the street from the opening to the gray building. I could see the school parking lot and the guardhouse. It was pretty boring just sitting there, but I was afraid that if I took out a book or something, I'd miss Mrs. Flannery leaving. Then I got a brilliant idea. If I could just sneak into the back of Mrs. Flannery's car and crouch down real low, I could easily find out where she was going. I'd be going right with her! And if she happened to go into the gray building, then I could get past the guard because he would never know I was there!

It was a brilliant plan, even if I did say so myself. I just wished Lori and Jeff could have been there to watch me put it in action. I stood up and walked toward the school parking lot. "Oh, please," I said to myself, "just don't let Mrs. Flannery come out and see me getting into her car." I got to the parking lot and kept watching the office door so that I could run if Mrs. Flannery came out. Pretty soon, I passed the white car that was three away from Mrs. Flannery's, the school van that was two cars down from Mrs. Flannery's, and the little red truck that was next to Mrs. Flannery's blue car. My heart was pounding so hard that I could hear it in my ears. I kept telling myself, "Just get to her car. Look around fast, and then put your hand on the back door and open it pronto. Pull the door shut behind you, and lie on the floor."

It sounded so easy but, as I reached Mrs. Flannery's blue car, my hands were shaking so hard that I wasn't sure I could open the door at all. Biting my lip hard, I reached for the metal handle and turned it. Out of the corner of my eye, I noticed that the front door of the school was opening, and I heard the click of a high heel. "Come on, open fast!" I whispered to the door, but nothing happened, and then suddenly, as Mrs. Flannery came into view, I realized that her car door was locked. Mrs. Flannery's high heels clicked their way closer to her car and to me.

Had she seen me trying to get into her car? I was dead. I wanted to run, I really did. With those high heels on, she couldn't possibly catch me, but I was frozen to the spot. It was a million years, or maybe it was only a minute, before her shrill voice barked, "Julia Rose Johnston, what are you doing next to my car?"

"Who me?" I squeaked.

She huffed, "Well, I certainly don't see any other child of that name near my car. Now, I repeat, what are you doing?"

"Doing?" I asked.

"Julia," she thundered, "when I ask you a question, I want it answered with an answer, not another question."

"Okay," I said, thinking frantically, "uh, you see, I can get extra credit in math if I count how many cars there are in the parking lot."

"And why is your hand on the door handle of my car?" Her beady little blue eyes stared at my hand, and I pulled it from the door.

"Uhh, I am keeping track of how many four-door cars there are and how many two-door cars. Then I'm going to make a chart and a graph, and uh, I'm going to show which kind of car is more popular at school." My words were rushing out and tumbling on top of each other.

Mrs. Flannery's blue high heel tapped on the sidewalk. "That is absolutely absurd. I'm — " Then she looked at her watch. "I don't have time to deal with you today, but I'd better never catch you near my car again, is that clear, Julia Rose?" She didn't wait for an answer, and there seemed to be a special kind of evil in her voice as she added, "It seems to me that you are causing far too much trouble for one child."

With that, she climbed into her car, slammed the door shut, started the motor, and drove from the parking lot. My legs were shaking so hard that I couldn't even follow her. I waited until she had turned out of the school lot, and then I sat down on the sidewalk right where I was. In a few minutes, my legs stopped feeling like puddles of jelly, and I hit my hand on the sidewalk. Why couldn't anything ever go right? All I had managed to do this afternoon was make Mrs. Flannery more suspicious.

I looked at my watch. It was still only four o'clock, an hour before I had to meet Lori and Jeff at our tree. I hated to have to face them with only the news that I had botched things up, so I decided to sit by the fence outside the gray building for a while. Even though I couldn't get in, maybe I could at least hear something that would be valuable. I walked out of the school grounds, wishing that Lori or Jeff were there. Somehow, things don't seem quite so scary when you're not alone.

When I got to the entrance to the gray building, I peeked in, hoping that maybe the guard wasn't there, but of course, he was. He came out of his little house, and he recognized me. "Go on, kid," he said. "I told you yesterday that you weren't allowed in here."

"Right," I said, "I'm going." But as I walked past, I noticed Mrs. Flannery's blue car parked near the entrance to the building. So she was here again! In spite of everything, I felt a tingling excitement. I knew it. I just knew she was in the middle of all this. Now if I could only find out what this was.

I sat down outside the gray wall. I couldn't see the guard, and I was sure he could no longer see me, but I could overhear faint sounds of a baseball game he must have been listening to on the radio. Then suddenly, I heard another man's voice. He and the guard were talking. The guard's deep voice grew louder. "No way the Cubs can take the Series."

"Ha," shouted the other voice. "Put your money where your mouth is. They'll not only do it, but they'll do it in five."

"You're on," said the guard.

"Put that in writing!" said the other voice.

"Come here a sec, and I will."

I peeked through the opening. The guard and another man in a uniform were bending over a table in the guardhouse. This was it! This was my chance. I crouched down low and hurried in. "Don't forget to write that they'll do it in five," said the voice as I scurried past the guard station.

I could hear their voices getting fainter as I ran toward the gray building itself. I tried not to think about what could happen if they caught me now. After all, it was only in the movies that they killed kids as spies, right?

Hearing footsteps, I ducked into one of the bushes by the front door of the gray building. The bushes had some kind of thorns on them, and they were pricking me everywhere. I had to suck in my breath and close my lips real tight to keep from shouting or moving. One of the voices said, "Oh, I don't believe it. I forgot my new code sheet. I wish they'd quit changing this thing every week."

"No problem," said the other voice. "This week's is easy for me; it's my birthday. Five-four-teen-fifty-two." I heard the door open and close, and then there was silence.

Peeking out of the bushes, I could see a button pad next to the front door. It looked just like the buttons on a telephone only it was bright blue with white numbers. I looked around. No one was coming. Saying a big thank-you for my good memory for numbers, I went to the button pad and pressed five-one-four-five-two. Then I put my hand on the silver door knob of the gray door and turned. It opened. I was actually inside the forbidden building.

10

Quick, I thought to myself, I'd better find a place to hide before someone finds me. In front of me was a wide, empty, gray hallway with gray doors. All the doors had silver handles, and all of them were exactly alike except for the black numbers in the center. There was no place to hide in the hallway, but I was afraid to open a door because I didn't know who, or what, was behind it.

I wished I could be taller and have some sort of a uniform on. My red T-shirt and jeans were going to stick out if anyone even glanced down the hallway. At least I was wearing my tennies so that my shoes wouldn't make noise on the gray cement floor.

There was a big sign on the wall. In black letters it said:

WARNING
IF YOU DO NOT HAVE SECURITY CLEARANCE
LEAVE THIS BUILDING IMMEDIATELY
AND REPORT TO THE FRONT GATE

Well, I'm not going back to the front gate, I thought, but I had to get somewhere fast because a shadow far down the hallway seemed to be moving my way.

I took a deep breath and blindly opened a door, hoping that no one with a gun was waiting on the other side. Barging in, I was almost afraid to open my eyes. Then I spotted the sink. "Oh, thank you, thank you," I whispered as I looked around at the empty bathroom. I went into one of the stalls and locked the door. At least, no one would be able to see me here. It felt so good to be safe. Who knew what was behind some of the other doors? Maybe I'd have walked into one of them and disappeared forever.

I stood in that bathroom stall for a long time. I was just stumped. I had worked so hard to get into this building that I didn't want to leave. I might never solve this mystery unless I explored this place. Then again, no one knew I was here. If I did end up in trouble, no one would find me. Not even Lori or Jeff would guess that I had been able to slip through the security at the front of the building.

What to do? I wouldn't leave, and I was afraid to go out in the hallway again, so for a long time I stood in the bathroom stall examining the gray door and hoping for a brilliant idea. My stomach started to growl, and I looked down at my watch.

It was almost six o'clock. I had to do something. I walked out of the stall, timidly opened the door to the hallway, and looked out. To my surprise, most of the lights were off. I hadn't stopped to think about it, but this building must have closed! I could hardly believe my good luck. I was alone, here to explore and find out the truth with no one to stop me or bother me!

My dumb stomach growled again, and I told it to be quiet because we had important work to do, and eating would come later. I began to open the gray doors up and down the hallway. Most of them looked pretty much the same. There were gray desks in them and gray filing cabinets. They sure didn't look very mysterious or even very interesting. I kept heading down the hallway. The sixth door on the left opened to reveal a much bigger office than the others. On the desk was a name plate that read COLONEL JOHN ROGERS. Next to that was a file that said EYES ONLY.

"Well," I said into the silence of the empty building. "I certainly have eyes." I opened the thick file folder and tried to read. So much for Miss Kendrick saying I was the best reader in the fifth grade. This stuff was impossible to understand. I didn't know there were this many big words in the whole world. There must have been at least a hundred pages in the report, but they all looked impossible. Then finally, after the last page was a scribbled note that I could under-stand. It said, *The bottom line is that after the field testing, this vanisher project just isn't work-ing. Not one thing has disappeared.*

I sucked my breath in and read the words again more slowly. But it had worked; it had worked on us! Why did they want things to disappear? And how was Mrs. Flannery part of this? And what was the vanisher project?

It had to be around here somewhere! "Vanisher project," I said to myself, looking at the file draw-ers behind the big desk. I put my hand on the drawer marked V-Z and pulled, but nothing hap-pened. It was locked. That only made me even more certain that there must be important stuff about the vanisher in that drawer, maybe even the machine itself!

I noticed that there was a silver letter opener on the desk with a big brown handle. I picked it up. Maybe there was a way to wedge it in the drawer and get the drawer to pop open. I tried sticking the pointed tip of the opener on the side of the drawer, but it wouldn't go in. Then I tried the top part. Pushing with all my strength, I shoved the letter opener into the drawer. My hands ached, and I felt out of breath, but I didn't care. If I could just move the letter opener over a little, it might push the lock down. I shoved as hard as I could, and suddenly I heard a snap. The handle of the letter opener was still in my hand,

and the rest of it was wedged firmly into the same spot on the drawer. "Darn it!" I called.

Then I heard a noise. Someone else was in the building. "Please, don't have noticed the light under the door of this office!" I silently prayed, making my shaking legs take me to the switch to turn it off. If the noise was heading this way, I had to find a hiding place fast. In the dark, the only place I could think of was under the desk. I scooted under and scrunched into a ball so that I fit. My heart was pounding so loud and so hard that I couldn't tell if there were still footsteps in the hallway or if it was just my heart hammering in my ears. I don't know how long I stayed frozen in a ball under the desk, sure that at any moment someone would burst in and discover me. But after what seemed like a long time, the sound in the hall was gone, and I crawled out from behind the desk and stood up. I was so shaky that I had to hold onto the chair to keep from falling down.

"That's it," I said to myself. It was just too scary to do this all by myself. I almost wished I had never gotten into this building. I would have been at home right now, where it was light, and safe, and I would have been eating dinner with my family. All of a sudden, tears just started rolling down my cheeks. I knew it was stupid to cry, but I couldn't help it.

I wanted to get out of here. Tomorrow, I could tell Lori and Jeff that there was such a thing as a vanisher project, that somehow it had been responsible for the class disappearing, and that . . . that I had been right in the same room with it and had been too chicken to stay until I found it.

I sighed. That dumb curious part of me that had to have answers wasn't going to let me leave this place yet. "So what now?" I asked myself. I walked over to the wall to lean against it and think.

After being scrunched up for so long, it felt wonderful to stretch out against the wall. I leaned my back against the wood to stretch my neck, and all of a sudden the whole wall began to turn around.

"Wait, stop," I squeaked as I felt myself being moved, but the wall continued to turn.

11

When it stopped, I was in another room, and in the middle of that room was a big gray machine. I sucked in my breath. The Vanisher! It had to be! Suddenly, I wasn't tired or scared or even hungry anymore. I just wanted to find out what it was and how it worked.

I remembered Miss Kendrick saying that real scientists took good notes on everything they did so they could study their experiments over and over again. That's what I would do with the Vanisher. Just like a real scientist, I would write down everything about this machine and what it did. I didn't want to forget this in my whole life. I took some paper off a gray table in the room, and I wrote, *"This room has no windows at all. There is only one door at the west end, and there is a secret wall that somehow when pressed leads into the room. In the middle of the room is a gray machine, which is just about as tall as I am. It looks a little like a big camera."*

Putting the paper down on the floor, I walked over toward the machine, but I didn't get too close. I wasn't sure if it somehow just turned on by itself, and I certainly didn't want to disappear forever. Squinting my eyes, I could make out the words on a button on the top. It said ON/OFF.

"Okay, Julia," I told myself bravely. "Just don't press the button, and you'll be okay."

I made myself walk around to the front of the Vanisher. There was a big piece of glass on the front that looked like the lens on my camera, only this one was rainbow-colored. It was so pretty! I wondered if it just unscrewed or something, and I could take it out to look at it better. Grabbing the outside of the silver part surrounding the rainbow glass, I tried to turn it. At first, nothing happened, but then I jumped up, grabbed it with all my might and turned really hard, and the glass bounced out of the machine.

"Oh, no!" I gasped, watching it fall. "Don't break!" But the glass rolled onto the ground before I could stop it. I held my breath as it spun on an edge and then fell to one side. I rushed over to it.

"Thank goodness!" I whispered as I saw that it was still in one piece. It was beautiful. From the brightest red at the top to the deepest violet at the bottom, colors had never looked so crystal clear or perfect.

I left the glass on the ground for a minute and

walked over to the opening that it had fit in. Closing one eye, I leaned in and tried to see what was behind the glass, but it only looked like a black hole. I went back to the piece of paper and wrote everything that had happened. As I read it back to myself, I thought it sounded great. Maybe I was really a pretty good scientist already!

I stared at the glass on the floor, and an idea began that made me smile. Why couldn't I just put the glass back into the machine, and turn the Vanisher on for just a minute? If it looked like a camera, and the lens came out of it just like a camera, then the disappearing picture had to be of what was in front of it, not behind it. I would be fine, as long as I stayed behind the button. "Come on," I encouraged myself, "don't be chicken. When will you ever get another chance to make something disappear?"

I walked back over to the glass, but when I tried to lift it up, I almost fell down. It looked so fragile, but it was a lot heavier than I had thought How would I ever get it back into the machine?

There just had to be a way. If only Lori and Jeff were here! The three of us could have lifted it easily. I looked around the room for something to help me, but the only other items besides the Vanisher were a small table and a chair. They would have to do. I pushed the table over toward the glass. Picking up one side of the glass, I tilted it so it leaned against the table, and then I held my breath as I tried to push the glass onto the top of the table without breaking it. Whew! It was done. Now, if I could just lean the glass up from the table onto the Vanisher and then push it into the opening. It sounded easy enough, but it was real hard to do. By the time I had pushed the glass in place, my T-shirt was all sweaty and my hands ached. Still, it was back in the opening. The only problem was that it didn't look like it was going to stay there very well. I must have bent the silver part a little when I took the lens out, because I couldn't get it to stay fastened around the glass.

Now what! I thought. Every time I was sure I had solved the problem, a new one was there. If only there was something in the room that I could use to tie the silver thing shut around the glass, but there was nothing. Suddenly, I remembered the copper wire I'd picked up in the playground at recess. I'd wound it into a little circle and stuck it in my pocket. Was it still there? I could only hope. My hand felt deep into my jeans pocket. "Yes!" I said happily to the empty room as I took out the wire. Winding it around the bent spot in the silver casing, I decided that the glass would now certainly stay in place.

Now, all I had to do was turn on the Vanisher, and that table in front of it would disappear. I, ten-year-old Julia Rose Johnston, would be one of the only people in the whole world who would have made something disappear! I could almost see my picture on the front page of *The Morning Herald*.

I walked to the back of the Vanisher. The button part was right above my shoulder. All I had to do was reach out and touch it. That was all. "Come on scaredy-cat!" I told myself. "Push the button already!"

My hand was shaking, but I reached out and pressed the button. It began to glow, and I held my breath as I stared at the table very carefully. One minute passed. Two minutes passed. Three minutes passed, and I began to wonder how long it took something to disappear. I looked at my watch then the table, and waited, but even after ten minutes, the table was still there. It hadn't even moved. Biting my lip, I tried to tell myself that I really hadn't expected it to work, and I turned the machine off.

Still, I knew it did work. Otherwise, my friends and I wouldn't have disappeared from school. Maybe, something was still loose from when I had pried the glass off. I walked around the front of the machine and tried to tighten the silver part that I had tied together with the wire. My hand reached up and began to twist the copper wire. That should help. I started to walk back to try the machine again, but all of a sudden I noticed that something real weird had happened to my hand. It was only sort of there. I mean I could see that I had a hand, but it was kind of a see-through ghost's hand. As I stared at it, I realized that the same thing was beginning to happen to my arm. With a really scary feeling, I put my other hand to my head to make sure it was okay, but my hand just sort of floated through it.

How could the Vanisher have done this when it was off. Who knew what else it could do? I didn't want to find out. I just wanted to get out. I began backing away from the machine. Without even realizing it, I was against a wall, only I wasn't exactly against it. I was sort of floating through it, only before I could do or say anything, I stopped floating halfway through it. I was caught in the middle of a wall. Half of me was on one side and half of me was on the other side. It didn't really hurt or anything. It was just so freaky. I was a ghost trapped in a wall.

I tried to be brave. I really did. I tried to tell myself that I was sure that it would all wear off in a few minutes, but I wasn't sure at all. In fact all I was sure of was that I wanted out of here. "Help!" I began to yell, wondering if anyone could even hear my voice. "Help me, please help me!"

12

I don't know whom I expected to answer. I certainly hadn't heard anyone in the building in a long time, but I kept screaming anyway. I couldn't stop. Then, just as I was about to give up hope, I heard a key in the door, and I watched as a uniformed man burst in. He was holding a gun, and that gun was pointed right at me. "Is that thing real?" I squeaked.

"Oh, my, #$@#$." He said a bunch of words my mom would never let me use. Then his eyes got real big. "What are you?" he barked. "You better give me some straight answers, or I'll . . . I'll shoot!"

"Don't do that," I sobbed. "I'm just a ten-year-old kid who's stuck in a wall. Please, get me out so I can go home."

The guard's eyes were still gigantic. "You don't look like any kid I ever saw." He flipped a walkie-talkie from his pocket. "This is Sergeant Fowles.

Get hold of Colonel Rogers and Dr. Shaner ASAP. Tell them Code Red, Project V."

Sergeant Fowles was scaring me with that gun. I didn't know if transparent people could get killed. "Uh . . . my name's Julia," I said. "I go to school next door at Sandhill, so you don't need your gun."

"I don't know what you are, but you aren't no real kid. That's for sure." Sergeant Fowles wouldn't say another word, and he didn't lower his gun. Pretty soon, two men came into the room. One was wearing a uniform with lots of medals on it. He had to be Colonel Rogers. The other one had a white laboratory coat on over a uniform. I guessed he was Dr. Shaner.

Sergeant Fowles put his gun away and saluted the two men. "Reporting in. All the intruder said was that it was a ten-year-old kid who went to Sandhill."

"Okay, Sergeant Fowles. You're dismissed," the man with the medals said, and the sergeant left. I was glad to see him and his gun go away.

"Please," I said, "I'm getting very stiff here halfway between two rooms. Could you please take me out?"

"A horrific breach of security," said Colonel Rogers.

"A remarkable phenomenon," said Dr. Shaner. The colonel turned to Dr. Shaner, "I suppose you have some scientific babble to explain all this."

"No, actually I don't at all." The scientist walked toward me. "Hi, I'm Dr. Shaner. What's your name?"

"Julia Rose Johnston," I replied.

The colonel broke in. "Right, and you're a ten-year-old kid who just happened to turn invisible and elude every bit of military security we have. Come on. Be honest with us, or you'll never get out of there. What are you really?"

"I am just a kid," I said, trying not to cry.

Dr. Shaner looked at me kindly. "I believe you, Julia, and I'll try to get you out of the wall, but I need to know how you got into it."

"Well," I sniffed and tried to wipe my nose with my hand, but my hand floated through half my nose and hit the wall. "It all started when my class at Sandhill kept disappearing." I told him how I'd figured out that something here must be causing it and how I'd come to find out. I told him about taking the glass lens out of the camera and then putting it back in and tying it with the copper wire. "I was real careful to turn the machine off before I touched it, but somehow it didn't make any difference."

"Amazing! Fascinating!" Dr. Shaner looked really excited.

Colonel Rogers looked mad. "Forget all the glowing words. What's it mean?"

Dr. Shaner smiled. "It means that my Vanisher, which you called a thirty-seven-million-dollar waste of money, works! It's worked all along. It's just that the aim was off.

"As to what happened in here tonight, I'm not sure. I'm going to try to get this child out of the wall, but I can't guarantee anything. I suggest you stand out in the hall unless you want to take a chance of ending up like her."

Colonel Rogers left the room and slammed the door behind him. I asked Dr. Shaner, "Do you really think you can get me out? Please say yes!" I begged. "And how come I didn't just disappear and then turn into a real person again like at school?"

Dr. Shaner tried to answer my questions as he began fiddling with the Vanisher. "The copper wire changed the electron focus field. It weakened it, but held it on the tip of the machine even after the machine was off." He went on about neutrons, and matter, and effects on force fields. Maybe it was because I was stuck in a wall, and only half there, or maybe it was just all too complicated, but I didn't understand most of what he explained. Finally, Dr. Shaner quit fiddling with the machine.

"Julia," he said, "you've been a very brave girl tonight. I'm going to turn the machine on now. I think it will make you completely invisible for just a minute, in which case you must immediately get into one room or the other. Do you understand?"

"Uh-huh," I said. "But what if it doesn't work?"

Dr. Shaner wouldn't answer me. "We've got to try," was all he said.

13

He undid the copper wire and moved it to the bottom of the machine. Then Dr. Shaner stood behind the ON/OFF button. I thought to myself, Oh, please let it work. I just can't stay stuck in this wall. Dr. Shaner pressed the button, and it began to glow. His voice seemed very far away as he called, "Jump, jump!" I wanted to ask him how on earth I could jump if I was still stuck in a wall, but something was happening to my voice, and I couldn't make any words come out.

Dr. Shaner turned the machine off, but I felt exactly the same. I tried not to cry as I thought about spending more time with the front of me in one room and the back of me in the room next door. They would have to show people through the building, and say, "Oh, yes, that girl. She's stuck in the wall, and no one can get her into either room. You can see the front half of her here, and the back half of her next door."

"Julia! Julia!" Dr. Shaner's voice seemed excited. "That was a great jump. Do you feel okay?"

"But I'm still . . ." I looked down at myself. I was back to being a whole person, and instead of being stuck in the wall, I was just leaning against it. "Wow!" I hugged myself, and it felt so good to have my solid hands and arms reach around my solid body. "Oh, thank you, Dr. Shaner. I'll never, ever forget you! You saved my life."

Dr. Shaner ran his hand through his curly red hair, and smiled, "Well, Julia, that makes us even, because you saved the Vanisher!"

I folded my arms across my chest because it felt so good to be solid again. "It's a real important discovery, isn't it?"

"It sure is. It's been my life and my dream for the past twenty years, and the army was about to scrap it. But because of tonight, and you, the research will go on."

"Wow," I said pretty impressed with myself. "What's the Vanisher for?"

Dr. Shaner's deep blue eyes got very serious. "In war, many people get hurt or killed. It can be quite terrible. But suppose if instead of killing the enemy troops, we could just make them disappear. Poof, and they're gone. We can return them to the same spot, or we can put them someplace altogether different. Either way, it means no more war." Dr. Shaner was getting more and more excited. "If no one can fire on our troops, no one can get hurt. Imagine that!"

"Wow! How does it work?"

Dr. Shaner explained the scientific principles, but I didn't understand most of what he said. Of course, that didn't mean I wasn't still filled with questions, like wanting to know why I hadn't disappeared that first time, and why he didn't know that our class was disappearing.

Dr. Shaner replied, "I didn't know your class was disappearing because they weren't the intended target. The reason the whole project was about to be branded a failure was that the targets we had set up and aimed for never disappeared at all. That's why the big brass decided that the machine didn't work." He stroked his chin. "Now, as to why you and your teacher didn't disappear with the rest of your class . . . I have several theories, but I can't say for sure. Obviously, the whole Vanisher needs more research in an isolated area where civilians can't be accidentally involved, but . . ." and then Dr. Shaner smiled and clapped his hands again, "the important thing is that it does work!"

Dr. Shaner and I talked a little longer. I told him that after hearing him, I was even more sure I would become a scientist when I grew up. I told him how the very first time the rest of the class had disappeared I had been daydreaming about winning the science fair. My eyes got big. "Gee, Dr. Shaner, do you think that my mind was so involved with science that I couldn't disappear?"

Dr. Shaner smiled. "Well, I'm not sure if day-dreaming about science kept you from disappearing, but what you've done here tonight Julia Rose Johnston has contributed a great deal to science and to the world. In fact, you may be a good part of the reason that no more people have to die in war." Dr. Shaner said it definitely wasn't too early for me to start working on a science career. We talked for a few more minutes and I told him how much I wanted to win this year's science fair. "No fifth grader has ever won the grand prize."

"Well, I'll bet all that changes this year," Dr. Shaner said. "A mind as curious as yours will be hard to beat."

Just as I was feeling that this was turning out to be just about the best night of my life, Colonel Rogers stormed through the door. "We've got more problems tonight." He glared at me. "Maybe we should have just left her in the wall. Bring her down to Room 4."

Colonel Rogers looked really mad. He took my arm, and the three of us walked in silence to Room 4.

14

As we neared Room 4, I tried to imagine what might be wrong now. Colonel Rogers opened the gray door and, as I looked in the room, my mouth dropped open. "Lori, Jeff!" I called excitedly to the two sad figures sitting on hard gray folding chairs. Sergeant Fowles was standing guard over them.

"See, I told you she was here," Jeff said defiantly, "and the whole police force will come here looking for us real soon, so you better not try anything." Lori's big brown eyes looked petrified, but she nodded in agreement.

Colonel Rogers banged on the desk. "Quiet!" he shouted to us. Then he muttered to Dr. Shaner, "I knew it was a bad idea to build this installation next door to a school. Intelligence said it was a perfect cover, an ordinary building that looked much too low-tech to be of interest to any spies. So instead, what do we have — a whole school yard of kids who've come to play junior detective."

Jeff was absolutely white and shaking, but he was trying to be real brave as he told Colonel Rogers, "And don't think you can get away with doing anything to us. We know all about you and Mrs. Flannery."

I took a deep breath. In all the excitement, I'd completely forgotten about Mrs. Flannery, but before I could say anything, Colonel Rogers barked, "Who in the devil is Mrs. Flannery?"

Sergeant Fowles answered, "Sir, I can tell you about Mrs. Flannery. She's the school secretary from next door. She has been driving the adjutant here crazy. Since we are a government institution, she believes it is our patriotic duty to provide a Veteran's Day program for the children. She called three times, though we tried to explain that we didn't do that sort of thing at this facility. Finally, she insisted on coming over and speaking to someone in proper authority. Colonel Miller was supposed to meet with her yesterday, but he got tied up in a meeting, and so she came back today. Of course, we didn't let her see anything confidential. In fact, I was the guard who was her escort while she was here." Sergeant Fowles turned to me, "Kid, I feel sorry for everyone at your school. What a witch!"

"Yeah, we call her Dragon Lady," I said. Then it hit me. "You mean Mrs. Flannery didn't have anything to do with our disappearing?" I had been so super sure that she was the key.

The guard shook his head. "She just kept talk-ing about the principal being sick and her having to plan this program for Veteran's Day."

Colonel Rogers said, "I can assure you that Mrs. Flannery was in no way associated with this fa-cility. Now, young lady, let's talk about how you and your friends got into this place?"

Dr. Shaner smiled at me, and I could tell that in spite of his tough tone, Colonel Rogers wasn't going to hurt us. I walked over to Lori and Jeff. "It's okay, you guys. They're just doing some im-portant stuff here, and they need to know how people could get in and out." I told Colonel Rogers how I'd gotten past the guard, overheard the code to get in, and then hidden in the rest room until everyone was gone. Lori and Jeff looked real im-pressed. "But how'd *you* guys get in?" I asked.

Lori said, "We got so worried about you when you didn't show up for our meeting that we figured they must have captured you here. So Jeff and I developed a plan. I talked to the guard so he wouldn't notice that Jeff was sneaking by. Then Jeff ran as fast as he could. He made it all the way to the door, but it was locked or something. He started banging into it, screaming for you, but you didn't come out, and the guard got us, and then he brought us here, and . . ." Lori's eyes filled with tears. "It's all been pretty scary."

"But it's all got such a great ending." I couldn't help but be excited. "You see Doctor Shaner has this special machine, and nobody has to die because of it, but he didn't mean to make us disappear."

"Hey," Jeff said, scratching his head, "could you slow down and explain this so that a person could understand it?"

"Okay," I said, "I was just so excited that . . ."

I'd been so happy that I didn't even notice the strange look in Colonel Roger's eyes. "Enough," he commanded. "Dr. Shaner, we have a major security leak here, and I am holding you personally responsible. There is no way that we can let three juveniles go around spreading one of the military's most classified secrets. I don't want to hurt any kids. You know that. But we cannot let them go. The country's safety won't allow it."

I expected Dr. Shaner to jump right in and defend us, but he didn't. In fact, he wouldn't even look at us. Suddenly, this room didn't feel so friendly anymore. In fact, it was uneasily silent. The uniformed man was probably planning how to kill us; I was figuring out how Lori, Jeff, and I could possibly escape, and Dr. Shaner was probably only thinking about his experiment.

I couldn't stand the silence anymore. It was too creepy. "Listen," I said, "we won't tell anybody what we saw or learned. If we don't tell anyone, isn't that as good as not knowing at all?"

Colonel Rogers frowned. "Look, it's nothing personal. It's just that we can't count on three children to keep one of our country's most important military research secrets. I'm afraid that they'll just have to permanently disappear."

Dr. Shaner looked at Colonel Rogers. "You're right that they may not keep our project a secret. They certainly haven't so far. In fact, Julia, didn't you tell me that as soon as you first saw your friends disappear from class, you told them all about it?"

I stared at Dr. Shaner, fighting back tears. How could he be betraying us this way? "But I didn't know it was an important military secret then, I mean . . ."

He interrupted. "You told Lori, Jeff, and even Mrs. Flannery right away. Now, what happened after you told them? Were they excited, scared?"

Suddenly, I realized what Dr. Shaner was trying to do. "No one believed me," I said.

"Exactly," Dr. Shaner turned to Colonel Rogers. "Suppose three ten-year-old kids tell you that the building next door to the school is filled with military men who are vaporizing the fifth-grade kids at the school. As a reasonable adult, what would you think?"

Colonel Rogers raised his bushy white eyebrows. "I would presume that the children were making up absurd scenarios and should be forced to stick to the truth."

"Exactly," Dr. Shaner said. "That's what any

reasonable adult would conclude. So you see, these kids are really no security threat at all. Let them say what they will. If they say anything at all, they'll only get in trouble for making up stories. Besides, I and the Vanisher will be long gone from here. I've got to work in an isolated area until I figure out the problems with the range of the machine."

Colonel Rogers shook his head. "This certainly is not standard operational procedure for security." He sighed deeply. "But it makes sense, I guess, and I've learned some things from these three, too. We'll definitely be instituting some new security procedures.

He turned to Sergeant Fowles. "Would you please escort these three children to the gate, and would you make absolutely certain that they have left." Then he turned to us and crossed his arms, "And you three better never come back here again, understood?"

"Yes, sir," we said in unison getting up quickly. "Just a minute," Dr. Shaner said. He walked over to me. "I'm really glad you came tonight, and I'm glad that you're thinking of becoming a scientist. Maybe, some day we'll even work together. Meanwhile, keep asking questions and following your curiosity. Never forget that scientists make the impossible possible!" He shook my hand just like I was a real grown-up.

"Thanks," I said. "I hope I get to do experiments as important as yours, and I'll never forget — "

"All right," Colonel Rogers interrupted. "Enough. Get these kids out of here." The guard walked us to the gate as he had been instructed, waited until we were outside, and pulled it firmly shut behind us. We ran down the block just to make sure we really had escaped, and then we hugged each other.

"We're alive!" Lori yelled.

"We're free!" Jeff screamed.

"And we were right!" I exclaimed.

15

As we stood there laughing, my stomach growled. "Wow, I just remembered that I'm starved, and . . ." I took a deep breath. "Oh, boy, am I ever in trouble. What time is it? I never showed up for dinner. I'll bet my mom is scared to death. She's probably called the police and everything."

"It's okay," Lori said. "Remember, you were supposed to eat dinner at my house tonight. When you didn't come, I figured you must be on the case, and so I told my mom you had decided to go home for dinner." Lori looked pretty pleased with herself. "Then my mom thought you were at your house, and your mom thought you were at my house, so no one's mom was upset. Except during dinner, I started thinking about it, and I got worried that something really had happened to you. So right after dinner, I called Jeff, and we went looking for you."

"Good thinking, Lori!" I was proud of my friend,

and I was glad that I hadn't scared anyone's mom. My stomach was growling nonstop now, and I told Lori and Jeff I had to get food. Pooling our money, we had $2.32, enough for a hot dog at the Stop and Shop on the corner. I practically inhaled it. Then as we walked home, I explained every detail of what I had learned from Dr. Shaner. Lori and Jeff gasped and oohed and ahhed. They were thrilled to find out that there really was a disappearing machine. They were amazed to learn that not only weren't we the intended victims, but no one had even known we'd disappeared. Like me, they couldn't believe that Mrs. Flannery hadn't been responsible for any of this. She hadn't even understood what was going on. "I guess," Jeff sighed, "that means that the school is still stuck with the old Dragon Lady!"

Lori giggled. "Can't you just see her marching up to those big important military guys telling them they had to put on a Veteran's Day assembly for us."

We talked and laughed until we dropped Lori off at her house, and Jeff and I split ways to walk to our own houses. When I opened the door, my mom was in the living room waiting for me. "You're almost a half-hour late," she said. And before I could answer, she added, "You know I don't like you out after eight-thirty, even if you were just under your meeting tree at Lori's."

"I'm sorry, Mom, I really am; it won't happen

again." I started for my room. Then my naturally curious part took over. I stopped and walked back over to Mom's chair. "What if I told you that I wasn't under Lori's tree at all, but that the real reason I was late was that I was exploring a machine that could make people disappear so that we wouldn't have any more war?"

My mom ran her hand through her dark hair and tried not to smile. "I would say that you have a wonderful imagination, but it's no substitute for the truth. Besides, making up stories will not excuse you from being late, and you know it! Now go to bed and enough nonsense!"

I thought of Dr. Shaner. He was right. No one would ever believe what had really happened. After that, I didn't say much about the whole night to anyone except Lori and Jeff. Once, after science, I stayed in during recess to ask Miss Kendrick if she thought it was possible for people to disappear. I was sure she had seen the class vanish before she fainted that one time. But Miss Kendrick only looked at me a little strangely and said, "Mrs. Flannery says that any such talk is absolute nonsense, and no one who plans to work with children should ever entertain such a thought." Then she changed the subject.

Every so often during recess, Lori, Jeff, and I would look across the playground at the military building. We'd catch each other's eye and smile, but we never tried to get in there again. We didn't dare risk running into Colonel Rogers with Dr. Shaner gone.

The school year moved on in a real normal way. Mr. Mac came back to school. Mrs. Flannery remained as dragonish as ever. Jeff still told a ton of dumb jokes. Our class never had anything exciting like a disappearance happen again and, after a while, our whole adventure almost seemed like a dream.

It had been the best, scariest time of my life. But it didn't make me or Lori or Jeff famous. Meanwhile, the science fair was getting closer and, even though Dr. Shaner had said my mind would be hard to beat, my mind couldn't think of a single project worth entering. Everything was either too dumb or too impossible. It didn't help that our school board had decided that this year's science fair should be a giant one open to all five schools in our district. When Lori heard that news, she decided that there would be too much competition for her to even bother entering. "Imagine! All the best science kids in the whole district. Good thing our school has you, Julia!"

Jeff said he didn't care about winning, but he needed the extra credit so he was going to do a report about his dead frog. He'd stuck it in formaldehyde to display it at the fair.

I kept wishing that somehow Dr. Shaner could have stayed here to help me because I really needed to win. I hadn't told anyone, but I had decided that if I couldn't even win my school science fair, I might as well give up trying to be a great scientist. It seemed like the harder I tried to find the perfect experiment, the more I couldn't find anything at all.

It was only three weeks before the science fair when Mrs. Flannery's voice squawked over the intercom. "Miss Kendrick, there's a package here for Julia Rose Johnston. Send her to get it at recess."

Walking to the office, I thought about the last time she had called me from class. Today, Mrs. Flannery looked up at me and frowned. "This came for you," she said, holding a large white envelope. "I am certain that children should not be receiving mail at school. There must be a rule about it somewhere." She sniffed with irritation, and her long red fingernails dropped the envelope into my hands.

I waited until I was out of the office to open it and then pulled out a book entitled *Scientists' Greatest Challenges*. I opened the book and on the inside page was written, *"Thanks again for everything. My experiments are finally going well; I hope yours will, too*. There was no signature, but I knew just whom the book was from. Dr. Shaner hadn't forgotten me after all.

That afternoon, I went home and read the book. It was awesome. The scientists were all different from one another, but all of them talked about never waiting for the perfect experiment. They just kept trying things because they were curious about what would happen.

I sighed. Maybe I had been so busy trying to win the science fair that I had forgotten how to be curious. I had sure been interested in Dr. Shaner's Vanisher. I had no idea how it worked, and I wasn't sure I ever would, but it was neat to think about it. Not that I was thinking of doing an experiment about the Vanisher. It was much too complicated. But maybe . . . I could do one on positive force fields. I could keep that pretty simple, and it might help me understand how I got stuck in the wall. All of a sudden, I started getting really excited. I could begin to see how neat my experiment could be, and I began to scribble some notes for myself.

Every day after school I worked a little more, and by the night before the science fair, my experiment looked pretty good. I had certainly learned a whole lot about molecules. In some ways, I almost understood how I had managed to partly disappear that day with the Vanisher.

I put the last of my report on the big blue and gold board I had made for my project and took it to school. Mom dropped me off, hugged me, and told me she thought it looked wonderful. I thought so, too, until I took it in the auditorium for judging. There were fifty-six other entries there, and at least half of them looked absolutely super.

The more I tried not to think about the awards ceremony, the more I couldn't think of anything else. I wished that somehow I could just go to sleep for the next three days until they announced the awards. Twice when Miss Kendrick called on me, I was daydreaming about the awards ceremony. When Lori asked me if I was getting excited, I practically took her head off. In fact, by the time the awards night came, I was pretty much of a wreck.

As we walked into the auditorium, I had butterflies the size of boulders in my stomach. It was still fifteen minutes before the awards were supposed to start, and there were almost no seats left in the whole auditorium. Lori waved to me and pointed to two seats she had saved for me and my mom. When I sat down, Lori squeezed my hand. "It's got to be good luck that the awards ceremony is at our school."

I wasn't feeling very lucky. In fact, my stomach was thinking real hard about throwing up the whole time that the president of the Board of Education for our district was talking about students and science. "And now, I am proud to announce the award winners for this year's expanded science fair. I will announce a winner from each grade level." His voice seemed to be coming through a fog.

"He's up to fourth grade, and none of the winners have been from Sandhill. It's got to be our turn when they get to fifth grade," whispered Lori.

My head was feeling like mushy cotton when the board president announced," And now for the fifth-grade winner . . . Julie . . ."

Lori grabbed my hand! "You did it! You did it!"

And the board president continued, ". . . Smitherton from Challenger Elementary School. Julie Smitherton's experiment was . . ."

Lori looked away, embarrassed, and I fought back tears. Jeff leaned over and whispered, "That dumb old trophy would just junk up your room anyway. Who wants it?"

Who wants it? I thought. *I* want it. I watched Julie Smitherton of Challenger Elementary School carry the big silver trophy off the stage, and I bit my lip. At least Dr. Shaner wasn't here to see that I was a failure.

I was so miserable that I barely even heard the sixth-grade winner being announced.

I stared at the one big gold trophy left on the stage for the grand prize winner and wished they'd hurry and award it to one of the grade winners so this evening would be over. Probably it would go to Julie Smitherton or the sixth-grade winner.

But the evening would not be hurried. Instead of just awarding the grand prize, the president of the board of education began talking more about the science fair and how pleased they had been with the quality and quantity of entries. "And now for the one prize left, the Alhambra District Grand Prize Winner for the overall most outstanding science fair project. . . ." When he actually said Julia Rose Johnston from Sandhill Elementary School, I was sure I must be dreaming. Then I heard Lori and Jeff shouting.

I turned to my mom, and tears were running down her cheeks. "Oh, honey, I'm so proud. Go get your award."

My wobbly legs somehow carried me to the front of the room and up onto the stage. I shook hands with the president of the Board of Education, and picked up the huge trophy. I smiled at Lori, Jeff, and my mom still applauding.

Suddenly, I had a strong feeling that even though he was supposed to be far away, Dr. Shaner was somehow here to see me get my trophy. "Thanks for all your help," I whispered into the air, and just then I was almost certain I heard a soft, "You're welcome," in reply.

About the Author

Terri Fields lives in Phoenix, Arizona, with her husband Rick and her children Lori and Jeffrey. A teacher who believes there are always magical mysteries and moments at school, she's also a prize-winning writer and the author of FOURTH GRADERS DON'T BELIEVE IN WITCHES.